Series 401
A Ladybird Book

PIGGLY PLAYS TRUANT is an exciting story in verse about two little pigs who played truant from school and had many lively adventures.

The full page colour plates reach a high standard of excellence, and will make an instant appeal to all children.

PIGGLY PLAYS TRUANT

Story and illustrations by
A. J. MACGREGOR

Verses by
W. PERRING

Publishers: Ladybird Books Ltd . Loughborough
© Ladybird Books Ltd (formerly Wills & Hepworth Ltd) 1947
Printed in England

Lazy little Piggly-Wriggly

    Often stayed in bed to snore

After Mother Pig had called him—

    For he always snored *before*.

4

0 7214 0209 7

Once upon a day young Piggly

    Stayed in bed an hour too late,

While his mother called and called him—

    Breakfast cold upon his plate!

Piggly washed, and gobbled breakfast,

    Packed his school books in a rush;

Hurried round in getting ready,

    Never gave his clothes a brush.

Dashed off quickly in a hurry,

    Lest he should be late for school;

It was five to nine already,

    He'd be half way, as a rule.

Soon he saw his playmate, Porky,

Half asleep and going slow;

Called to him, and Porky waited—

Porky didn't want to go!

Porky showed him, from his pocket,

Coloured marbles, shiny—new ;

Piggly took a little handful

And his eyes were shiny, too.

They forgot about the master,

They forgot about the class;

Played at marbles on the roadway—

On the roadway, not the grass.

Till a shiny coloured marble,

Knocked by Piggly out of reach,

Rolled and bounced across the cliff-top

Out and down upon the beach.

Down they climbed upon the seashore,

Searched in vain : then had a rest.

Piggly saw the boats and shouted,

" Sitting in a boat is best ! "

But to reach them wasn't easy.

Then they found a tree nearby,

Broke a branch off for a boat hook—

Piggly had to reach up high!

So they dragged the nearest boat in

After very many tries,

And with many slips and splashes—

Quite forgetting how time flies!

Climbing in was quite a struggle;

    Little Porky, very wet,

Said, " Oh, what about the master? "

    Piggly answered, " Don't go yet! "

So they rested in the sunshine,

    And they thought it splendid fun

When the fishes said " Good morning ! "—

    But the boat went floating on !

Came the seagulls, screaming, sailing,

Piggly-Wriggly tried to row—

School and master quite forgotten—

Porky steered them to and fro.

Later on they had their lunches,

Greedy Piggly didn't think—

Left his oars—while busy eating,

Having lemonade to drink.

Over went an oar and floated

On the tide till out of reach,

Seagull came and stood and watched them

Drifting further from the beach.

Porky took their spotted hankies,

Tied them on the other oar,

Hoping somebody would see them—

Still they drifted from the shore.

But the oar was very tiring,

    Till they could no longer stand;

Now the sun began a-sinking—

    They could hardly see the land.

Old Salt Pork upon his lighthouse

    Took his telescope to see;

Saw the oar and spotted hankies,

    " That must be a wreck ! " said he.

So he went and filled a basket

    With the things he meant to take;

Apples, cups, a flask of cocoa,

    Then some biscuits, and some cake.

In his boat he put the basket

    And some blankets; on the mast

Tied aloft a lighted lantern,

    Then he started off at last.

Soon he reached the sorry Piglets,

    Helped them clamber in with him;

Shivering, but not so frightened—

    Now they wouldn't have to swim.

Then he wrapped them in the blankets

    And he tied their boat behind;

Turned and rowed towards the lighthouse—

    Old Salt Pork was *very* kind.

Telephoning to their parents—
    Parents fetched them home to bed,
Where they sniffed and sneezed and
                                snuffled,
    Eyes a-streaming, noses red.

Medicine and water bottles
    Hung around them all the day—
That's the sort of thing that happens
    When a youngster stops to play.